Almost
Katharine the Great

Major Mama Drama

by Lisa Mullarkey
illustrated by Phyllis Harris

magic wagon

visit us at www.abdopublishing.com

To Carol and Rose: Two per-fect-o, fab-u-lo-so moms!—LM

To the two mothers in my life. My wonderful mother, Ellen, and also my wonderful mother-in-law, Barbara —PH

Published by Magic Wagon, a division of the ABDO Group, 8000 West 78th Street, Edina, Minnesota 55439. Copyright © 2009 by Abdo Consulting Group, Inc. International copyrights reserved in all countries. All rights reserved. No part of this book may be reproduced in any form without written permission from the publisher.

Calico Chapter Books™ is a trademark and logo of Magic Wagon.

Printed in the United States.

Text by Lisa Mullarkey
Illustrations by Phyllis Harris
Edited by Stephanie Hedlund and Rochelle Baltzer
Interior layout and design by Jaime Martens
Cover design by Jaime Martens

Library of Congress Cataloging-in-Publication Data

Mullarkey, Lisa.
  Major mama drama / by Lisa Mullarkey ; illustrated by Phyllis Harris.
    p. cm. -- (Katharine the almost great ; bk. 2)
  ISBN 978-1-60270-580-7
  [1. Mothers and daughters--Fiction. 2. Schools--Fiction.] I. Harris, Phyllis, 1962- ill. II. Title.
  PZ7.M91148Maj 2009
  [E]--dc22
                                             2008036089

❋ CONTENTS ❋

❀ CHAPTER 1 ❀

Super-Duper ~~Secret~~ DUD

I'm a super-duper secret keeper. Except when the secret is so big, it just puffs up inside my mouth until it explodes-a-rooni.

Maybe that's why my parents call me Katharine the *Almost* Great. They say I'm a work-in-progress. I bet if I could zip my lips and keep the cat *in* the bag, they'd finally crown me Katharine the Great.

The last time I spilled the beans was when Aunt Chrissy bought my cousin Crockett a skateboard for his birthday.

"Don't let the cat out of the bag, Katharine," said Aunt Chrissy. "No blabbing."

"Me?" I asked in my very most innocent voice.

I kept the secret for a whole entire day. But then Crockett's lizard, Hercules, died. Crockett got Hercules from his dad right before his parents got divorced. He saw Hercules a lot more than his dad. So, losing Hercules made Crockett miss his dad even more.

Crockett said Hercules needed a funeral. He dug a hole in the yard and buried him with three dead crickets. He even wrote a poem. It went:

> *To Hercules my lizard,*
> *you had the best gizzard.*
> *You lived through a blizzard.*
> *If I were a wizard,*
> *you'd still me my lizard.*

The poem was per-fect-o.

Crockett's voice cracked as he read it and he sniffed . . . a lot. I'm a good friend and a great cousin because when he snuffled all that gunk, I didn't even tell him how disgust-o it was.

I wanted to cheer him up and knew exactly how to do it. I blurted, "Guess what you're getting for your birthday."

"What?"

Then I thought of Aunt Chrissy. I didn't want to be a blabbermouth, so I covered my mouth with both hands and shook my head.

"I can't tell you," I said in a muffled voice. "It's a secret."

He shrugged and wrote *R.I.P. Hercules* in the dirt with a twig.

That twig gave me an idea. I wouldn't *tell* him. I'd *show* him. Having a blabber*hand* is much better than being a blabber*mouth*, isn't it?

I used the twig to sketch a skateboard on top of Hercules's grave. As soon as I added wheels, Crockett's eyes lit up.

He jumped up and down. "I'm getting a skateboard?"

I nodded but got twitchy. Then itchy. Then my mouth had a little explode-a-rama drama.

"A-red-one-with-lightning-bolts-on-top-and-Tony-Hawk's-autograph-on-the-bottom." I sucked in my breath. "Don't tell anyone. It's our secret."

But who knew Crockett had loose lips? When he opened his present after dinner, he looked confused. "It's blue, Katharine. Not red."

I mouthed *sorry* to Aunt Chrissy and skedaddled out of that room fast. After that, no one told me a secret for a long time—months even.

So during breakfast today, I hugged Dad when he said that Mom had a secret to share.

"Is it a super-duper secret?" I asked.

He gave me two thumbs-up.

Wow! I did a happy dance. I was starting to think no one would ever share another super-duper secret with me. And that would have been too bad because how can I practice my secret keeping without super-duper secrets?

But I had to wait until Mom got back from her walk with my little brother, Jack.

After I zip-a-zoomed through breakfast, I jumped three times in front of the sink area. That's my signal for Crockett to come upstairs. He lives with Aunt Chrissy in our basement.

A minute later, Crockett bounced up the steps. "I heard your mom has a secret."

"A super-duper secret," I said.

When Mom came home, she rubbed her hands together and announced she had big news. She said "big news" in her thundery voice.

This is what I wanted her to say:

"You know how we've talked about going on vacation to Florida to visit the mouse and his friends? Well, pack your bags because in just a few days, you'll be wearing your purplicious princess dress and dancing with Prince Charming."

But this is what my mom really said:

"I'm going back to work part-time as the new cook in your cafeteria!" She whipped a chef's hat out from behind her back and plopped it on her head. "Isn't it great?"

My stomach did a flip-flop belly drop. I glanced at Crockett. He had a big goof-a-roo grin on his face.

I *tried* to smile. I *tried* to look happy. Luckily, I have a calendar filled with 365 useless facts that come in handy for times like this.

"Did you know that there are approximately 3 million gallons of water in the moat that surrounds Cinderella Castle?" I wanted to add, *the castle we will NOT be visiting anytime soon.* But I didn't. I used my common sense.

Mom cocked her head to the side. "Aren't you excited, Katharine?" She pulled a cookbook off the counter. "You can help me plan menus. Maybe give me ideas for desserts."

She flipped through the pages. "We're going to have so much fun together!"

Fun? Was it *fun* when she spied pudding cups on the back table during our poetry reading and told Mrs. Bingsley that chocolate pudding gave me diarrhea? Nope.

Was it *fun* the time she volunteered in the library and gave me a saliva bath after seeing marker on my cheek? Nope.

Mom continued, "We'll have fun seeing each other during your lunch period. Won't we?"

I was doomed. My days of trading cookies and pickle sandwiches for

Matthew Jacob's Fluffer-Nutter peanut butter sandwiches were kaput.

"Won't it be fun when we bump into each other in the hallway?"

Double doomed. She'll discover *all* my "visits" to the principal.

It was NOT a super-duper secret. It was a super-duper dud.

She was getting ready for fun.

Me? I was getting ready for major mama drama.

❊ CHAPTER 2 ❊

A Sour Day

The next morning, I skim-a-rooed my Monday morning Do Not Forget checklist on the fridge.

Ugh! How could I forget?

At ten thirty, the door to my classroom opened and Mom's head poked in. "Good morning, Mrs. Bingsley. I have your milk and muffins for snack."

"Mrs. Carmichael! Welcome, welcome." She motioned for Mom to come in.

"Katharine, why didn't you tell us your mom is working here at Liberty Corner? I found out this morning."

I shrugged. Mom followed Mrs. Bingsley's eyes to me. "Oh, there you are! Hi, Sweetie Pie! Are you working hard?"

She slid the milk crate in the door and waved. "I'll see all of you at lunch in a few hours, okey dokey?"

After she closed the door, she crouched down to peek back in through the glass. When she saw me looking, she blew me a kiss.

Vanessa, aka Miss Priss-A-Poo, turned around and blew a kiss too. Then she mouthed, "Okey dokey, Sweetie Pie?"

Before I had time to give her my grumpy face, I heard someone gag.

It was Crockett. "This milk is disgusting." He ran to the water fountain.

Johnny Mazzaratti opened his carton and took a whiff. "Oh, man. Nasty."

Vanessa walked over to Johnny's desk and scooped up the carton. After a quick sniff, she announced, "It's sour." Then she put her hands on her hips, scrunched her nose, and pointed to me. "Your mom gave us *sour* milk."

This is what I wanted to say:

"It matches the look on your face, Miss Priss-A-Poo Sour Puss Face Milk Girl."

But this is what I really said:

"Sorry."

Mrs. Bingsley opened another carton and hesitated before sniffing. Her face wrinkled up. "They're all sour." She turned toward Vanessa.

"According to the date on top, this milk should be good for several more days. Mrs. Carmichael couldn't possibly have known they spoiled." She poured the milk into the sink. "The refrigerator must be on the fritz again."

I blurted out, "Did you know that a cow's spots are like snowflakes? No two have the same pattern."

Mrs. Bingsley winked at me.

Lunch wasn't much better.

When I walked into the cafeteria, I spied my mom standing near the cashier. She was wearing her Flour Power apron and talking to Mrs. Ammer, our principal.

I crossed my fingers and thought, *Please don't mention my visit to your office on Friday.*

Even if I didn't see my mom, I could tell she was there because the place *looked* different. The condiment tables had plastic tablecloths. Wicker baskets with apples, bananas, and oranges were scattered around the room. Above the cashier's table was the sign she painted last night: *You Are What You Eat.*

Before my mom saw me, I rushed over to my seat.

Matthew's Fluffer-Nutter peanut butter sandwich was waiting for me.

"Wanna trade?" he asked. He had figured out in second grade that kids loved Fluffer-Nutter sandwiches as much as he did. So, he'd bring two and trade one to whoever had chocolate chip cookies or pickles, which was usually me.

I peeked in my bag. "I have tuna with pickles. *Lots* of pickles." I slid it over to him.

Miss Priss-A-Poo plopped her tray down and sat across from Johnny. "I just saw your mom, Katharine. She said to say, 'Hi, Sweetie Pie.'" She took a bite of her chicken finger, blew me a kiss, and fluttered her fingers the exact way my mom did this morning. "Okey dokey?"

Then Vanessa shrieked, "What are these? Where are my french fries?"

Crockett glanced over at her plate. "Those are french fries, right Katharine?"

I nodded as I watched my mom bounce from table to table handing out little white cups. Every once in a while, she'd turn, point to me, and wave. "They're potato wedges."

My mom thought regular french fries were greasy and full of fat. I was zipping my lips extra tight on that one.

But Crockett wasn't. "My aunt thinks fries are evil. I heard her tell my mom last night that she won't make them here."

I elbowed him. Now who was the blabbermouth?

Miss Priss-A-Poo scrunched her arms over her chest. "Yuck. These potato thingies probably taste *sour*."

Johnny grabbed a wedge off of Vanessa's plate and shoved it in his mouth. "Not bad." He swiped another. "Actually, pretty good."

Just as I swallowed the last piece of my sandwich, Mom bounced over to our table.

"Hey, kids, these are for your potato wedges." She tilted a tray filled with dozens of little white cups toward us. "Dip your fries in one of these for a little extra kick. You can have BBQ sauce or mango salsa."

She smiled, then leaned over and gave me a quick peck on the cheek. "Hi, Sweetie Pie. How's your day so far?"

My face turned as dark as the BBQ sauce in Miss Priss-A-Poo's little white cup.

She glanced down at my lunch bag. "You've finished your lunch already? Did you like the extra pickles in the tuna today?"

Before I answered, Miss Priss-A-Poo piped up. "Katharine never eats the food you send, Mrs. Carmichael. She trades her food for Matthew's Fluffer-Nutter peanut butter sandwiches." Then she looked at me and smiled. "Every day."

Mom's eyes got bulgy. If she didn't have to finish passing out those little white cups, I knew she'd get mega thundery with me. "We'll talk at home, Katharine."

I slumped down in my seat and watched Vanessa lick the BBQ sauce of off her fingers.

I flicked a crumb at her.

I should have known that Miss Priss-A-Poo couldn't keep secrets either.

❀ CHAPTER 3 ❀

Too Many Cooks in the Kitchen

W hen I got home from school, Aunt Chrissy was playing *This Little Piggy* with Jack's toes. I kissed him on the cheek and whispered, "You're lucky Mom's not making baby food for all of your friends."

"How was your mom's first day?" asked Aunt Chrissy.

I shrugged and handed Jack his elephant rattle.

Aunt Chrissy picked up a diaper. "She left a message on the machine and said she'd be home around dinnertime. She wants to settle in a bit."

Did getting settled mean getting to know the other people who work at school better? What if Mr. Ray told her I had four overdue library books? What if Mrs. Fields told her I forgot to wear sneakers three times this month in gym? My head hurt.

After Crockett and I finished our homework, he wanted to feed his lizards and play with his creepy crawlers. Since his tarantula, snakes, and lizards pretty much freak me out, I went to my room instead.

Then I grabbed a blank piece of paper and wrote:

RULES FOR MOM

1. No kisses (or blowing them) at school.

2. Check milk every day.

3. Leave snacks in the hallway just like Miss Karen did.

4. If you talk to Mrs. Ammer, don't believe everything she says about me.

5. Call me Katharine. Or Katharine the Super-Duper Great. But not Sweetie Pie.

6. Only say "okey dokey" to Jack.

I scanned my list and thought I had better add another after seeing my mom's eyes get bulgy today.

7. Don't use thundery words at school.

I taped the list to the mirror in her bathroom.

When Mom finally got home, she dropped a crinkly brown paper bag on the table and announced, "Dinner."

Dad sniffed the air. "It smells good, Carol. What is it?"

This is what I wanted her to say:

"It's Chinese food from Wing Li's. I asked them to throw in extra fortune cookies for everyone!"

But this is what she really said:

"It's leftovers from school today. We're having chicken fingers, potato wedges, corn, and rolls." She rifled through the bag.

"We're having *cafeteria* food for dinner?" I asked. "*Leftover* cafeteria food?"

"I don't want to waste it, Sweetie Pie," she said matter-of-factly. "It was tasty, wasn't it? Even Vanessa finally agreed the potato wedges were delicious."

The thought of Miss Priss-A-Poo *almost* made me lose my appetite.

Mom didn't stop talking about Liberty Corner the entire time we ate.

"Katharine, did you know that I'll save the school $50 a year by switching brands of ketchup?" she asked. "The one I found is all-natural. That extra money can go toward fresh fruit. Isn't that great?"

Not if you liked to eat those little cherries in the fruit cocktail cups, I thought.

She kept talking. "I was thinking of having a fresh fruit bar once a week with sliced pineapple and watermelon . . . maybe some kiwi. What do you think?"

She didn't wait for my answer.

"Maybe we'll have theme days." She buttered her roll. "Like when it's Dr. Seuss's birthday, I'll whip up green eggs and ham. What do you think?"

She didn't wait for my answer to that question either.

"Don't the first graders go on a class trip to the circus? I could have a circus theme with . . ."

"Mom," I squealed, "they're baby themes." I pointed to Jack. "Like goo-goo ga-ga."

Dad gave me the look. "Do you have any better ideas?" His voice wasn't quite thundery yet, but his face was definitely getting cloudy.

I wiped my mouth. "Did you know that P.T. Barnum purchased Jumbo the Elephant from the London Zoo in 1882 for $10,000?"

Jack burped. Everyone laughed, but then Mom got serious. "I'd love your input, Katharine. Like I said, you could help plan menus."

This was my chance. "How about a Super Bowl theme in January? And for Halloween, you could use some of the recipes from *Roald Dahl's Revolting Recipes* cookbook."

"Great ideas," said Mom as she grabbed a pad of paper and a pen. "Keep them coming."

I thought of scout camp. "We could have a campfire day with chili, corn bread, and s'mores."

She licked her lips.

I was going in for the kill. "Maybe you could let us pick chocolate milk or white milk for snack?"

"Sorry about the milk today. It's an old fridge." She scribbled down *choc milk*.

Maybe this wouldn't be so bad. "Can we have those fruit cups at least one day a week?"

She looked up. "But it's not *fresh* fruit."

I gave her my puppy dog eyes.

"Okay, once in a while won't hurt anyone."

Wow. She agreed to everything. "How about an ice cream sundae bar for special occasions?"

Dad spoke up. "That's a fun idea."

I wasn't sure if Mom liked my idea, but she wrote it down anyway.

That's when I got my best idea. A better-than-all-the-rest idea. "Why don't we have a recipe contest? Kids can make their favorite lunch and the winner will get to have it on the menu."

Mom shrieked. "What a great idea, Katharine. Kids will love it! They can drop off their samples in the cafeteria one day. Mrs. Ammer can judge." She wrote faster. "You've come up with so many fabulous ideas."

And I was starting to *feel* fab-u-lo-so because I knew that my bagel with strawberry cream cheese and jam blasts would win first place! I could almost hear Mrs. Ammer announcing my name on the intercom . . .

Mom interrupted my thoughts. "Guess what I'm making tomorrow?

Bagels with strawberry cream cheese and jam. The kids will love them."

I jumped out of my chair. "You can't. That's the recipe I'm entering."

My parents looked confused. Then Mom winced. "Katharine, I'll be judging the contest, so you can't enter. It wouldn't be fair."

My stomach did a flip-flop belly drop. It was my idea and what do I get?

Heartburn.

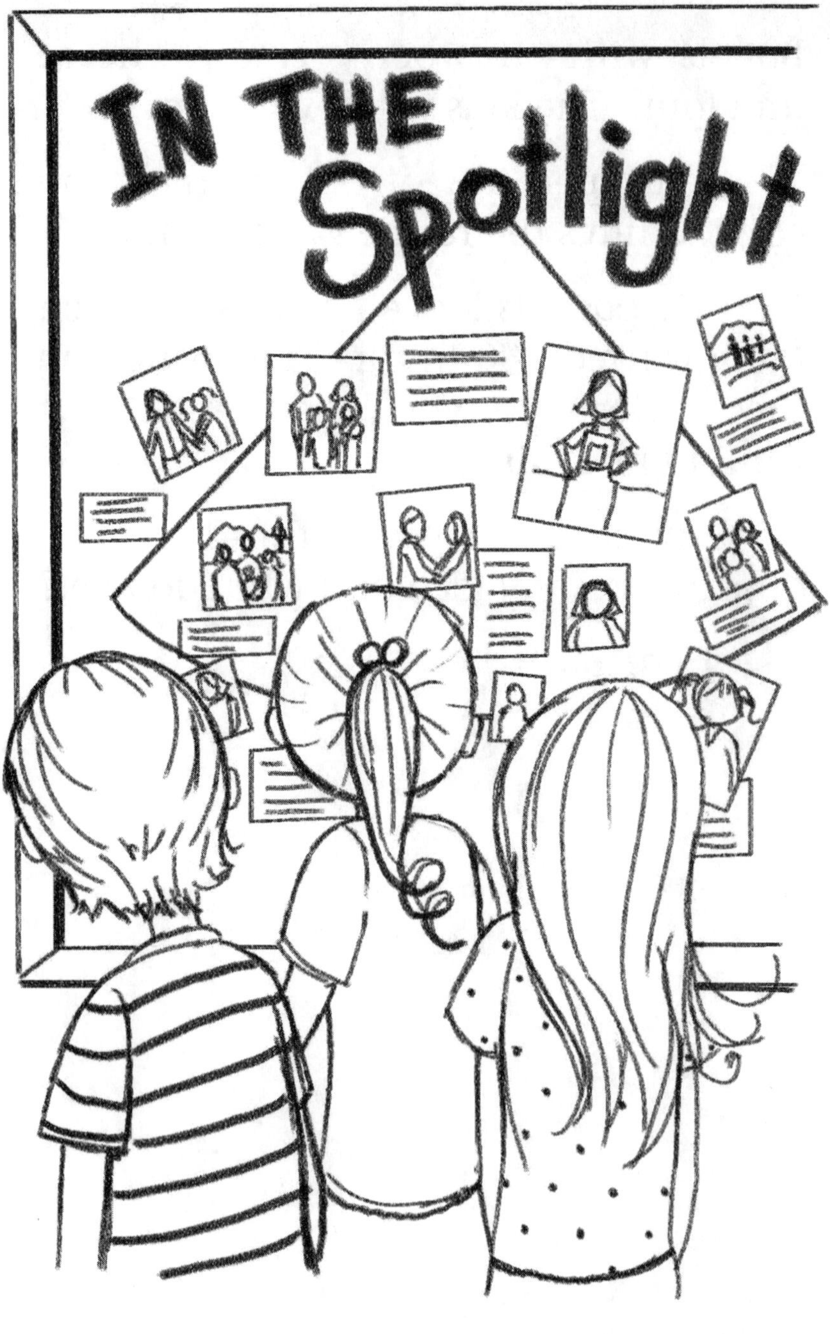
IN THE
Spotlight

❀ **CHAPTER 4** ❀

Lobster Girl Gets Crabby

Whenvec I woke up the next morning, I spied a note on my nightstand.

Dear Katharine,

> *I know you've been at Liberty Corner School a lot longer than me. I'm just starting to learn the ropes. It's tough having to learn the kitchen rules and your rules but I'll try, Sweetie Pie! (I can still call you that at home, right?) When the contest is announced, you'll get all the credit because it was your idea. Today will be a better day. Promise.*

> *Love, Mom*

The day started okay and even moved up to good for a while. There were no kisses, no disgust-o milk, no calling me Sweetie Pie in front of my friends. When I asked for a roll in the lunch line, Mom started to say *okey dokey* but switched to *coming right up* just in time.

I grumped a little when I saw my bagel with strawberry cream cheese and jam blasts crammed in mouths all over the lunchroom. They would have won the contest for sure.

When the contest was announced, my day cranked up to *almost* great. Everyone cheered and thought it was a per-fect-o idea. Especially Mrs. Bingsley.

"Kudos to you, Katharine," she said. "You have another winning idea."

But then the last period of the day came and my day turned as sour as the milk from yesterday's snack. Our class was shuffling down the hallway to gym when the line jerked to a halt.

Mrs. Bingsley squinted up at the *In the Spotlight* bulletin board. There were always goofy pictures and stories about teachers and workers at Liberty Corner. "Hey, kids, guess who's featured." She didn't wait for an answer. "Katharine's mom!"

I groaned at the thought of my mom putting goofy pictures of herself up where everyone could see them.

Everyone rushed forward to get a peek-a-roo. Except me. From my angle, I was able to see the picture of my mom wearing her Flour Power apron and making the peace sign with her fingers.

Every few seconds, I heard an explosion of giggles and whispers. It was a funny picture but not *that* funny. My stomach jumbled as I tried to think of the goofy pictures Mom might have sent.

Vanessa broke free from the crowd and pushed her way out to where I stood. "Don't you want to look, Lobster Girl?"

Lobster Girl?

Tamara laughed. "Did you get blistery that day? Last time I had that much sunburn, oozy stuff came out of me for days."

Before I had time to think, Johnny walked over. "I loved Bertie the Clown, too . . . when I was a baby."

I winced as I remembered the last few *In the Spotlight* bulletin boards. There were family pictures, too. Oodles and oodles of them.

"So you're still into Bertie, huh?" said Miss Priss-A-Poo as she glanced at Tamara.

I tried to think fast. "I took Jack. He likes him." They didn't need to know that I took him to cover up the fact that

I loved Bertie's magic tricks and thought his balloon animals were the best in New Jersey.

There was only one picture of me and Bertie and that was *supposed* to be in Jack's baby book. How could my mom put it here for the whole world—or at least everyone at Liberty Corner School—to see?

I got an icky feeling. An I-want-to-hide-my-face-and-scream feeling.

Mrs. Bingsley clapped her hands twice. "We need to get moving so we're not late for Mrs. Fields."

With that, the show was over. For my class at least.

When the line started moving, I dropped to the back and let everyone pass. Miss Priss-A-Poo glided by and pretended to suck her thumb. In a goo-goo ga-ga voice she babbled, "Babies like Bertie."

I put my hands on my hips. "Then you must be in love with him."

Crockett laughed. Vanessa stuck her tongue out at me and huffed away.

I ducked behind a display case and waited until the kids and Mrs. Bingsley had turned the corner before moving in for a closer look.

No wonder everyone laughed! The display was packed with about a dozen pictures, and I looked gross-a-rooni in half of them!

I looked at the beach one first. I'm slurping an ice cream cone and my face is burnt to a crisp. It's lollipop red. Fire truck red. Stop sign red. Way, *way* too red. Except for the snowy white ice cream beard.

On the bottom, the picture of me and Jack at Bertie the Clown's summer concert stood out. The worst part? I was hugging Bertie! Across from that was our family Easter picture with all of us wearing crazy carrot sunglasses and bunny pajamas. Ugh!

I had to get rid of the pictures before the rest of the school saw them. I scanned the hallway and when the coast was clear, I yanked Lobster Girl off first.

I heard a ripping sound and before I knew it, was staring at a four-inch hole in the paper. Next, I tugged on the Easter picture and then said *adios* to Bertie before snatching three more pictures of me and Jack.

Mission accomplished. But now the display looked lopsided. I scurried to the kindergarten room about 15 feet away and untaped a few of the paper apples off their door. Then, I retaped them to the *In the Spotlight* display. Just as I stuffed the last picture in my pocket, someone came barreling around the corner.

It was *Ammer the Hammer*. I was nailed again.

❄ **CHAPTER 5** ❄

The Pot Boils Over

Mrs. Ammer looked me up and down. "Katharine Carmichael. What brings you to the front hallway when you should be in gym with your class?"

I had to think fast. "Did you know that you only have to exercise 30 minutes a day, three times a week, to improve your physical fitness?"

She patted her tummy. "Good to know." Then she motioned toward the bulletin board and frowned. "This display looks . . . interesting, doesn't it?"

When I looked at the bulletin board, I pretended it was the first time I was seeing it. "Oh, wow! My mom's featured on the *In the Spotlight*? What a surprise!" Then I squinted, pretending to read the words under her Flour Power picture.

"My mom is such a super-duper interesting person, isn't she?" I'm a fab-u-lo-so actress, so I glanced at my pretend watch and acted like it was time to go. "Gotta go."

"Not so fast, Katharine." Mrs. Ammer picked up an apple that had fluttered to the floor. "I wonder who took down the picture of Bertie the Clown." Then she paused. "And I would love to know why this bulletin board is suddenly sprouting apples."

I gave her my very most surprised look as another apple drifted to the floor. "Bertie's picture was up there?" And then I gave another per-fect-o performance as I looked under a table.

Then for effect, I searched around the water fountain and shrugged. "I don't see him. Are you sure he was here?"

But the look on Ammer the Hammer's face told me that I should have left the clowning around to Bertie. "I hung this bulletin board up about an hour ago so I should know. Besides, my grandson loves Bertie."

She took a deep breath and twirled the apple in her hand before swiping the remaining apples off of the board. "It disheartens me to see that someone has *defaced* school property."

She used her thundery voice when she said "defaced."

I had no clue what defaced meant. But I was smart enough to know that I must have done the defacing and was in trouble. The no-dessert-for-a-year kind of trouble. The no-birthday-parties-forever kind of trouble. The no-playing-with-Crockett-after-school-or-on-weekends kind of trouble.

Mrs. Ammer pointed to her office. This is what I wanted her to say:

"I think I'll go inside and track down the guilty party. Tell Mrs. Fields I said hello."

But this is what she really said:

"We need to chat in my office. Now."

When I sat down on her purplicious chair, Mrs. Ammer tapped her desk. "Put the pictures here."

I stood and wrestled the crumpled pictures out of my jeans. Lobster Girl was on top. "Sorry."

"And why would you deface property, Katharine?"

I shrugged.

Mrs. Ammer sighed. "You do know what defacing means, don't you?"

I shook my head.

She pulled a dictionary off of her desk, flipped through some pages and read: "Deface: To intentionally spoil the appearance of something."

I put my head down on her desk. "I didn't want to spoil anything. I was just trying to make it look better. Honest."

Then, I told her all about how super hard it is to have your mom work in your school if she blows you kisses and calls you Sweetie Pie. Then I blabbered about how Bertie was private and no one was supposed to see that picture. And then I jabbered on about the sour milk and Miss Priss-A-Poo.

Mrs. Ammer took notes. "It has been a challenging few days for you, Katharine. Anything else?"

Then I spilled my guts about the recipe contest and how I was positively positive that my bagel blasts would have won first place.

Mrs. Ammer licked her lips. "Do you mean that the bagels from lunch today were *your* recipe?"

I nodded. "I make them all the time. Sometimes I add blueberries or bananas."

She leaned forward and scribbled some more. After a minute, she said, "It's true you can't enter the contest. Imagine if you won. People would think your mom played favorites. You wouldn't want that, would you?"

I thought of Miss Priss-A-Poo. If I entered, she'd most likely start flinging notes at me calling me Cheatie Girl. I did not want anyone to call me Cheatie Girl.

A tear dripped. Then dropped.

Mrs. Ammer handed me a tissue. "But since the recipe contest was your idea, shouldn't you judge it?"

I hopped off the purplicious chair. "You mean it? Me? Be a judge?" A picture of me wearing a VIP sticker and walking around the cafeteria with a clipboard flashed in my mind.

"I don't see why not. After tasting your creation, you're certainly qualified. But," said Mrs. Ammer, "we still have to deal with . . . the incident."

I bit my lip and crossed my fingers. The last time I visited Mrs. Ammer, she said we'd keep that visit private. "Do you have to tell my mom about this visit?"

She pushed her chair out, stood, and shook her head. I rushed around the desk and hugged her tight.

She pointed to the door. "*I* don't have to tell your mom."

I turned around and saw Mom in the office.

Mrs. Ammer nudged me forward. "But you do."

❀ CHAPTER 6 ❀

To The Dungeon!

"Y ou what?" asked Mom leaning in closer.

"I de-de*headed* school property," I said glancing at Mrs. Ammer. She shook her head and pointed to her nose.

"I de*nosed* school property?" Mrs. Ammer's head shook faster.

Mom folded her arms.

Mrs. Ammer spoke up. "What she's trying to say, Mrs. Carmichael, is that she *defaced* school property."

Mom sucked in her breath and yelped. She quickly covered her mouth and sat in the chair which didn't look so purplicious anymore. I was positively positive Mom would use thunder and lightning words with me.

But she didn't. She patted the seat next to her. "Sit down, Katharine. Start at the beginning."

So I did.

Mrs. Ammer sat and nodded but didn't make a peep-a-roo until I finished. "Katharine, why don't you go to gym now? I want to speak to your mother privately."

I stood and blew my nose for the bajillinth time.

"Katharine," whispered Mom.

I was hoping she'd say this:

"Let's pretend this never happened."

But she didn't say anything. She did something way better. She hugged me.

At home, we didn't talk about my visit to Mrs. Ammer until I climbed into bed.

"You have to fix the bulletin board, Katharine. And you need to write a letter of apology to Mrs. Ammer. And . . .," She paused. "I'm sorry I hung up a picture of you and Bertie. I wasn't thinking."

I wanted to tell her that she must not have been thinking when she whipped out my Lobster Girl and bunny pictures either. But I zipped my lips and used my common sense instead.

She tucked me in. "In the morning, we need to get to school early and put up a new *In the Spotlight* board. Crockett will have to walk to school with Aunt Chrissy." And then she added, "We'll need new pictures, won't we?"

I nodded.

"How about you pick them out after breakfast and I'll help you hang them?" She kissed my forehead.

"That's my only punishment?" *Easy breezy,* I thought as I slid my hands under the covers and crossed my fingers.

"You're not getting off that easy," explained Mom. "After we fix the bulletin board, you're going to come into the cafeteria and help me prepare lunch for the kids."

"Really? That's not a bad punishment."

"Who said anything about it being a punishment?" She fluffed my pillow. "If you're going to help me judge the recipe contest on Sunday, I figured you'd better see how the kitchen works."

I sprung up in bed. "You're really going to let me judge the contest?"

"It was your idea, wasn't it?" she said as she turned off the light.

After we refaced school property with super-duper cool pictures of Jack and me, we headed toward the cafeteria.

"We need to go to the basement and get paper plates first," said Mom.

I sucked in my breath. "You mean *The Dungeon*?" I couldn't believe my luck. "You're taking me to *The Dungeon*?"

Mom laughed. "That's what all the cafeteria aides call it, too."

Didn't she know that's what *everyone* called it?

Last year, Johnny explained to everyone on the playground that The Dungeon was where Ammer the Hammer kept the *really, really* bad kids. I figured that defacing school property only made me bad, not *really, really* bad.

"Are we allowed down there?" I whispered. I was dying to see who the *really, really* bad kids were. Then I thought of Johnny. He would flip-a-roo when he found out that I got to see the really, really bad kids . . . or what was left of them.

"From what I understand," said Mom, "I'll be going down a few times a week for supplies."

We walked to the end of the fourth grade hallway. A door was marked *FORBIDDEN. Do Not Enter.* Mom pushed it open and stopped at the top of a flight of stairs.

"Wait!" I screamed. My stomach did a flip-flop belly drop. "Maybe we should get Mr. Bollwage." Mr. Bollwage was our custodian. He wasn't afraid of anything. Once I overheard him tell Mrs. Bingsley that he was going to use a snake to unclog a toilet in the boys' bathroom. I am very afraid of snakes, but not Mr. Bollwage.

"Come on," Mom said. She grabbed my hand. Before I had time to call out Mr. Bollwage's name, we were in *The Dungeon.*

And you know what? The Dungeon was not dark and dingy like a real dungeon. It was just one dusty, musty room filled with shelves and shelves of supplies.

No kids. Not even leftovers.

"You look disappointed," said Mom. "What were you expecting?"

I picked up a box of erasers off the floor. "Nothing really."

She grabbed a huge stack of paper plates and walked toward the stairs. But that's when I uncovered a box. And what I found inside was way more super-duper than anything I had expected to find.

❀ CHAPTER 7 ❀

A Special Delivery

I blew the dust off the yellowed, must-o smelling book. There was a picture of our school on the front cover.

Mom peeked over my shoulder. "It's a Liberty Corner School Cookbook from 25 years ago." She tapped the price in the corner. "They sold it for 50¢."

I flipped it over. "It says *Made with 3 Cups of Love, A Dash of Kindness, and a Heaping Teaspoon of Enthusiasm by the staff and students at Liberty Corner School.*"

I tossed the book to Mom. She thumbed through the pages and laughed.

"Here's an applesauce muffin recipe from Mrs. Ammer when she was still a teacher." Mom showed me the entry. "It says *From the Kitchen of Mrs. Ammer.* I think I'll make them on Monday and surprise her."

That's when I got an idea. A just-as-good-as-a-recipe-contest idea. "Why don't we make another Liberty Corner cookbook? Anyone who enters the recipe contest can have their recipe inside. Maybe the teachers will give us recipes, too."

"That sounds like a fun idea, Katharine."

Then I got another per-fect-o idea. "Maybe Mrs. Ammer will let us sell the cookbooks and donate the money."

Mom's eyes lit up. "The Food Bank will be thrilled!"

As excited as I was, I forgot all about the cookbook as soon as we trudged upstairs and I saw the cafeteria's kitchen. Rows and rows of pots and pans lined the walls. Gadgets were piled on the counters. "Mom, how come everything seems supersized?" I asked.

"They need to be, Katharine," said Mom. "After all, we cook for hundreds of people."

I spent the next 45 minutes helping my mom use the jumbo mixer to make tuna salad, arrange apples and pears in wicker baskets, and make spiced cookies. When they came out of the oven, she let me have a few.

"What's this?" I asked as I shoved the last bite into my mouth. Something shiny was poking out from under a blue cloth.

"Take a peek," said Mom. "It was delivered yesterday."

I yanked the cloth off of a silver box about the size of my desk. Two white tubes poked out the bottom. One was labeled White, the other Chocolate. "Are these for milk?"

"You betcha," said Mom. "It's an extra dispenser that the high school didn't want anymore." She wiped it down with a cloth. "You wanted chocolate milk so . . .," She flapped both hands toward the machine. "Ta-da!"

And the morning got even better. When I had to go to the bathroom, Mom let me use the one that said "Employees Only." There was a big brown basket filled with lots of smelly soaps and perfumes. I sprayed Citrus Mist on my wrist-a-roo. Yum.

A few minutes later, the bell rang. "You better get going," said Mom. "Thanks for all of your help." She handed me a box of fresh-baked cookies. "These are extras for your class. Tell Mrs. Bingsley they're nut-free." Then she grabbed a package of plastic spoons. "Can you deliver these to the teacher's room first?"

Could this day get any better? My class has wanted to see the inside of the teacher's room ever since our kindergarten teacher, Mrs. Curtin, told us about it.

Mrs. Curtin wore her bunny slippers in school every day. She said they were comfy and her real shoes were stuck under her bed in the teacher's room. Then she told us stories about the video games, candy machines, flat screen TVs, and even the disco ball that hung from the ceiling.

I thought about The Dungeon, the cookbook, the mixers and blenders, the milk machine, and the bathroom. Having my mom work at school wasn't all bad. I skip-a-rooed up to her and planted a big kiss on her cheek. "Bye, Sweetie Pie," I said.

I plopped the spoons on top of the cookie box and practically ran down the hall.

"Where are you going?" Miss Priss-A-Poo asked as she walked in the front door.

I kept on walking. "To the teacher's room, where else?" I acted like I go in there all the time.

"Kids aren't allowed in there," she reminded me.

I showed her the spoons. "I work here sometimes, so I'm an employee. I have a delivery."

Then I added, "Besides, I feel like playing a video game." I held up my wrist for her to smell. "I get to use the teacher perfume from the employee bathroom, too."

When I got to the door, I looked back to see if Miss Priss-A-Poo was watching. She sure was! I opened the door and let it slam behind me.

I looked around. Mrs. Fields was on the phone and waved. Where were the beds? Candy machines? Games? It was just a small room with tables, chairs, a refrigerator, and a microwave. No TV. No sparkly disco ball. Nothing.

Then I laughed. Mrs. Curtin sure did trick us!

When I came out of the room, Miss Priss-A-Poo was waiting by the water fountain. "Well, how was it?"

I was going to tell her the truth. But this is what I said:

"The TV is even bigger than I thought, but it's messy in there. Mrs. Fields is playing Astro Blaster. The beds aren't made yet and Mrs. Curtin has a whole closet for clothes. She sleeps in there every night." Then I leaned closer, "Mrs. Fields told me that Mrs. Curtin has a snoring problem."

Just then, Mrs. Curtin walked by in her bunny slippers and yawned, "Morning, girls."

Miss Priss-A-Poo and I giggled and made it to our classroom just before the final bell rang.

✿ CHAPTER 8 ✿

And the Winner Is . . .

Being the recipe judge gave me a flip-flop opposite weekend. Mrs. Ammer told everyone that discussing recipes with the judges could get you disqualified.

Crockett was a worrywart. He stayed in the basement all weekend and was afraid to look at me. When I asked him to go over to our neighbor Melissa's house with Jack on Saturday, he said, "Sorry, Katharine. No can do."

Crockett acted like I had killer Katherine cooties. He wouldn't talk to me or even look at me. He made his mom call me to nix our Friday Night Movie Fest.

So, when I called downstairs on Saturday, I was surprised when he answered the phone. "Hi Crockett," was all I got out before he shrieked and dropped the phone. Aunt Chrissy picked it up and said Crocket was sorry but he couldn't talk to me.

So it was me, Mom, Dad, and Jack all weekend. How much fun can you have with a baby who eats, poops, and sleeps most of the day?

Before I left for the contest, I pulled my hair into a super-duper tight bun. I wore my very best skirt even though it had a teeny tiny spaghetti stain on it. I searched through my lip glosses until I found Luscious Lemon Meringue Pie. I slathered it on, smacked my lips together, and blew myself a kiss in the mirror.

When I went downstairs, Mom handed me a box. "If you don't like this one, I have a plain one you can wear."

Inside was a Flour Power apron that was just my size. "It's fab-u-lo-so, Mom." I hugged her. "We'll be twins."

We pulled into the parking lot at four o'clock and parked next to Mrs. Ammer, who was getting out of her car.

She waved. "All the recipes should be here by now. The directions said that Mrs. Bingsley needed entries by three thirty so we wouldn't see who brought what."

As we walked through the cafeteria doors, a mishmash of smells smacked us in the face. There were oodles and oodles of paper plates with all sorts of cutesy food on them.

Mom spread her arms wide. "I bet there are more than a hundred recipes in this room."

Good thing I had skipped dessert!

Mom gave each one of us a clipboard and reviewed the directions: Mrs. Ammer and I would rate the taste, appearance, and originality of each recipe from 1 to 5. Mom would score its nutritional value. Whoever scored the highest in all categories would win.

"Remember," Mom said, "there aren't any names on the plates. Just numbers to keep eveyone's identity a secret."

Since I'm not such a super-duper secret keeper, I thought that was a per-fect-o rule.

"Ready?" asked Mrs. Ammer. "Katharine, you start here at number one. I'll take the middle." Then she looked at Mom. "Carol, you should start at the far end." She waved her clipboard in the air. "Bon appétit!"

I spent two hours nibbling, crunching, slurping, and munching my way through the entries. Some were good. Some were not so good. One made me gag-a-rooni. Sixteen got a zero for originality. Since when is a PB&J sandwich original? So far, a chicken taco with ranch dressing was winning. But then I got to #113.

On the center of a checkered paper plate was an English muffin. I lifted the top and saw a perfectly round egg sandwich with specks of orange and brown inside. Even though it was cold, the cheddar cheese and sausage tasted yummy.

Next to the sandwich were two pancakes rolled up and a small white cup filled with syrup for dipping. There was a little potato patty and a small cup filled with mandarin oranges and banana slices. *Breakfast for Lunch,* I thought. *Cool.* It earned a perfect score of 15 from me.

And I wasn't the only one who loved it. Mrs. Ammer gave it a perfect score, too. Mom rated it a four for nutritional value. "It could be a five if we use egg whites and low fat cheese."

After two hours, we had a winner. The only problem was, none of us knew exactly who the winner was.

Mom wrote down *113* on a slip of paper and handed it to Mrs. Bingsley. Mrs. Bingsley looked at the number, ran her finger down the list, and smiled.

She wrote the winner's name on the slip of paper and gave it to Mrs. Ammer.

Then we all went into the gym, where everyone was waiting to hear the results.

"Before we announce the winner," said Mrs. Ammer, "I want to tell everyone that you're all winners."

Everyone cheered and clapped. The kids in the crowd moved closer to the stage.

"Since all of the recipes were tasty, we're going to make a cookbook, include all of your recipes, and sell it. All proceeds will go to the Food Bank." The clapping started again. "And I'd like to thank Katharine Carmichael for that idea."

I bowed.

Mrs. Ammer continued. "And because this contest was Katharine's idea, I'd like her to have the honor of announcing the winner." She slipped the folded paper into my hand.

I closed my eyes and thought of Crockett. I hoped he was the one who came up with the breakfast for lunch idea.

I leaned into the microphone, unfolded the paper and cleared my throat. "And the winner is . . .," I glanced down and couldn't believe my eyes. "VANESSA GARFINKLE!"

Miss Priss-A-Poo ran up onto the stage and started blowing kisses to the crowd.

Mom inched over to me. "Vanessa, huh?" She put her arm around my shoulder and squeezed me tight.

I smiled and clapped extra hard for Vanessa and her recipe. She deserved to win.

A minute later, I looked for my mom and saw her getting her picture taken with Mrs. Bingsley, Mrs. Ammer, and Vanessa. Mom waved me over and made room for me.

Vanessa won the contest. But after all my mama drama, I was pretty sure that *I* was the biggest winner of them all.

A Recipe for Starting a School Cookbook

A school cookbook is a per-fect-o way to raise money! You can also get your community involved in this fab-u-lo-so character education project. Here's what you need to do:

1. Elect a group to plan and design the cookbook. Be sure to get adults as well as kids from each grade involved.

2. Decide how many cookbooks you will need to sell and the price of each book.

3. Gather as many recipes as you can from students, teachers, parents, and community members. Be sure to set a deadline so everyone knows when they need to get their recipes in!

4. Organize your recipes any way the group decides. You can put desserts first (yummy!) or name the sections with goof-a-rooni names.

5. Have an adult in the group work with a printer to get your cookbook published. Then sell them and donate a portion of the money to your local food bank!